凝光初現
FIRST RAY of LIGHT

華 文 俳 句 集
CHINESE HAIKU
ANTHOLOGY

郭 至 卿
Kuo Chih Ching

序一

相同於日本「俳句大學」的國際學部，以提倡「切」與「兩項對照組合」的二行華文俳句個人詩集「凝光初現」的台灣出版是值得慶賀的。

俳句原是日本的傳統詩型之一，現已跨越日文藩籬，在世界各地以不同的語言書寫，儼然成為國際性的文學型式。然而，綜觀國際俳句的實況即可理解，大部分的國際俳句都寫成三行，卻無表現俳句美學的實質內容。這是因為國際俳句對於俳句的形式與特色沒有達成共識所致。

為了於華文圈提倡俳句的本質「切」與「兩項對照組合」，並推廣俳句，我擔當顧問及作者參與洪郁芬、郭至卿、趙紹球、吳衛峰於二○一八年十二月《華文俳句選》的出版。除此之外，也擔當成立於二○一八年十二月四日的「華文俳句社」的顧問，力圖華文俳句的推廣與發展。

003

身為「華文俳句社」的顧問，我相當樂見郭至卿出版《凝光初現》俳句集。希望此俳句集的出版能使讀者更理解「切」與「兩項對照組合」的俳句美學，並冀望華文俳句能與古典詩、現代詩、小詩、散文詩等齊聚一堂共同豐富華文詩壇。

第一次認識郭至卿，是藉由她寫的俳句「女孩銀鈴的笑聲／春天的花園」。我給她的評語是「好俳句」。她似乎因此得到激勵，加入書寫俳句的行列。在不斷嘗試的過程，似乎愈來愈能體會俳句使用一個季語來捕捉生活瞬間美感的奧妙。

從這本俳句集的內容，如「詩人執筆的手不停啊！／春潮」或是「星月夜／閱讀探險家的小說」等佳句可窺見，她喜愛閱讀，並有出眾的文學素養和才華。我於此介紹幾首至卿刊登於熊本月刊誌的俳句。

「一聲雷／成績單上的紅字」大概是打雷時登記成績單的景象。雷的光和成績單的紅色構成鮮明的色彩對比。

「拄著枴杖的老人／聽北風」乍看之下，「老人」與「北風」似乎沒有直接的關聯。雖然如此，我們仍然能感受那老人拄著拐杖，彷彿正在對抗寒冷的北風而凜然站立的姿態。

「春光／未加框的風景畫」的春光於此處意味著「春天耀眼、柔和的光」。使

004

用措辭「未加框」，清楚描繪了春天一望無垠、日麗風清的山野景觀。「一聲雷」的色彩對比相當出色。「拄著柺杖的老人」的俳句中，「老人」與「北風」有不即不離、恰到好處的關係。「春光」的俳句使用「寫生」的技巧。這些俳句都使用「切」與「兩項對照組合」，都是相較於日本俳句有過之而無不及的佳作。

最後於此列舉幾首我心所慕的俳句：

窗外盛開的紫藤
愛情小說

坐岸邊的老人揮釣桿
水亦暖

春雨
閱讀連載的愛情小說

寒晴

救援隊傳來的消息

寒流至

二次大戰的紀念碑

日本俳句協會副會長、日本俳句大學校長、俳人

令和元年七月吉日

永田満徳

永田満徳先生簡歷

俳人、日本俳句協會副會長、俳人協會熊本縣分部長、日本俳人協會幹事、日本俳句大學校長、雜誌《未來圖》同人、雜誌《火神》總編輯。由恩師引領開始創作俳句三十年至今。在文學研究方面，著有對三島由紀夫和夏目漱石俳句的論考。

著有《寒祭》（文學の森），《漱石熊本百句》（合著，創風出版），《新くまも

と歲時記》（合著，熊本日日新聞社）。

序一

日本の「俳句大学」の国際俳句学部が提唱している「切れ」と「取り合わせ」を取り入れた二行俳句の華文圏初めての個人句集『凝光初現』が台湾で出版されることは大変喜ばしいことである。

俳句は日本の伝統的な詩の一つである。今では世界各地でそれぞれの言葉で書かれている国際的な文学形式である。しかし、三行書きにしただけの俳句は形式のみで、俳句の美学を表現しているとは思えない。それは俳句の型と俳句の特色に対する共通認識がないからである。

そこで、日本俳句の大切な美学である「切れ」と「取り合わせ」の二行書きの俳句を提唱し、華文圏での俳句の発展に寄与するため、私は顧問および作者として洪郁芬、郭至卿、趙紹球、呉衛峰と共に二〇一八年十二月に台北で《華文俳句選》を出版した。さらに二〇一八年十二月四日に創立した「華文俳句社」の顧問

009

になり、華文俳句のさらなる進展を図ってきた。

郭至卿氏が句集『凝光初現』を出版することは「華文俳句社」の顧問として楽しみである。なぜならば、この句集によって、「切れ」と「取り合わせ」の俳句の美学に対する理解が深まり、絶句（漢詩）、現代詩、短詩、散文詩などの様々なジャンルを持つ華文詩の中で、華文俳句の定着と広まりがより一層華文詩界を豊かにすることが期待されるからである。

私が初めて郭至卿氏に注目した華文俳句は「女子の銀鈴のような笑い声／春野原」である。郭至卿氏はこの評価によって励まされ、それ以来華文俳句を書き続けて、試行錯誤の中、季語一つで瞬間の感動を書き留める俳句の奥深さがだんだん分かってきたという。

郭至卿氏は本句集に収録されている「詩人の筆は止まらない／春の潮」や「星月夜／探検家の小説を読む」の秀句にも見受けられるように、大変な読書家で、文学的素養と才能は飛び抜けている。例えば、「くまがわ春秋」に取り上げた句を紹介してみよう。

「雷鳴一つ／通信簿の赤字」は雷の時に成績をつける情景であろう。雷の光と

通信簿の赤が素晴らしい色の対比を成している。

「杖で立つ老人／北風吹く」は「老人」と「北風」とは直接的には無関係かもしれない。しかし、寒い北風に抗うように、杖一本を突いている老人の凛とした態度が感じ取れる。

「春の光／額縁のなき風景画」は「春光」はここでは「春のまばゆく、柔らかな光」のこと。。「額縁なき」という措辞に、見渡す限り広々とした野山の美しい春景色が描き出されている。

「雷鳴一つ」の句は色の「対比」が見事である。また、「杖で立つ老人」は「老人」と「北風」とを即かず離れず取り合わせている。さらに「春の光」の句は俳句の技巧である「写生」が効いている。いずれも、「切れ」と「取り合わせ」を用いていて、日本の俳句に勝るとも劣らない句ばかりである。

最後に心惹かれる句を取り上げておきたい。

　　窓外に溢れんばかりの藤

　恋愛小説

011

岸辺の老人は釣竿を振る

水温む

春の雨

シリーズの恋愛小説を読む

遠雷

サスペンスの終わり

午後の居眠り

チリリンとアイスクリームワゴン

星月夜

探検家の小説を読む

驚嘆符の台北一〇一ビル

秋の空

秋の海

車椅子で遠方を見る老人

寒日和

救援隊のお知らせ

寒波来る

第二次大戦の記念碑

令和元年七月吉日

日本俳句協会副会長、日本俳句大学学長、俳人

永田満徳

013

永田満徳氏プロフィール

俳人、日本俳句協会副会長、俳人協会熊本県支部長、俳人協会幹事、日本俳句大学学長、「未来図」同人、「火神」編集長。恩師の紹介で俳句を始めて三十年、現在に至る。文学研究では三島由紀夫や夏目漱石の俳句などの論考がある。句集に『寒祭』（文學の森）共著に『漱石熊本百句』（創風出版）『新くまもと歳時記』（熊本日日新聞社）。

014

序二

俳句對生活忙碌的現代人來說，是一個可以稍微放慢腳步、停下來的理由。

詩人說：詩是跳舞。我說俳句是以文字展現光。生活中不特別追求，舉目所見內心的聯想、感動，以兩行、幾個字表達瞬間的光芒。俳句吸引我的是質樸的氣質，令人慧心一笑、自然、不做作的文字書寫。二、三年前我開始寫現代詩。有別於現代詩，俳句截取瞬間的感動，直白的用名詞書寫，對我來說是項挑戰[1]。在不斷嘗試的過程，越來越體會俳句用一個季語，在季節裡捕捉生活瞬間感動的奧妙。

在學習的過程，得知俳句的發展已在世界各國蔚為風潮。俳句不只是日本的生活藝術。國際上如法國的保羅路易・庫舒（Paul-Louis Couchoud）、艾茲拉・龐德（Ezra Pound）等意象主義詩人、墨西哥的諾貝爾獎得主奧克塔維奧・帕斯（Octavio Paz）、近年的諾貝爾獎詩人，瑞典的托馬斯・特蘭斯特羅默（Thomas

Tranströmer）也都書寫俳句[2]。而「Haiku Column」上參與俳句書寫的，有來自英、美、法、義大利、比利時、羅馬尼亞、匈牙利、加拿大、印度、巴基斯坦、台灣等詩人[3]。總而言之，俳句發展的全球化已超乎我們想像。

台灣的俳句發展源於戰前、戰時的日文教育。十多年前，受日式教育的已故黃靈芝先生獲得了愛媛縣的正岡子規國際俳句獎[4]。黃靈芝先生和十字詩創始人詹冰之後的台灣俳句，或漢語俳句，以一行十個字的減字定型方式外，有的以日文俳句，有的以五七五形式書寫。除此之外，還有將三行新詩稱為俳句的俳句新詩[5]。

中國漢俳創辦人之一林林先生也主張，漢俳不能只有五七五的型式。內涵必需接近日文俳句[8][9]。而五七五和三行或季語是否真能表達日文俳句的精神，有待思考[10]。日本俳人五島高資的論文[11][12]指出，國際俳句最重要的應是「切」，而不是季語或五七五的型式。因為有些國家四季同一個季節。而且語言有獨自的韻律。

俳句因英、日文音節差異，行數有一、二行的俳句，但以三行為主流[6][7]。

Writing and Enjoying Haiku 書中，六個英文俳句的第二點規則[13][14]提到：「俳句形式上最重要的是意義要分兩部分，因為俳句不能斷成三段，或只有一個平鋪直敘的句子。中間要有一個斷或休息，使一句俳句成為兩部分。」二〇一八年十二月出版

的《華文俳句選》更是以「切」和「二項對照」實踐俳句本質。有關台灣或華文俳句的發展較詳盡介紹請參考《華文俳句選》[15]。

撰寫這一百首俳句的過程，華文俳句社社長、資深俳人洪郁芬女士給我極大的鼓勵與建議，有她的耐心和大力支持，我才能完成這本俳句集。非常感謝洪郁芬女士！

這本《凝光初現》，以中、英、日，三種語言呈現，是在國際上推廣俳句的一個開始。想把學習結果與心得分享給已經寫俳句和還不知道俳句的大眾。也希望能引起不同語言的讀者更多關注，比起其他的文學形式，希望能帶領讀者在生活中重新領會最單純的美感。人人寫俳句是一種不花錢、隨手可得的藝術生活方式。

二〇一九年五月吉日

郭至卿

參考文獻

1　吳衛峰《華文俳句選》，台北市，釀出版，二〇一八年，十三頁。

2　川本皓嗣《華文俳句選》，台北市，釀出版，二〇一八年，三頁。

3　永田滿德《華文俳句選》，台北市，釀出版，二〇一八年，一百五十一頁。

4 川本皓嗣《華文俳句選》，台北市，釀出版，二○一八年，四頁。

5 洪郁芬《華文俳句選》，台北市，釀出版，二○一八年，一百四十頁。

6 Bruce Rose ed.,*HAIKU MOMENT. USA*:Tuttle Publishing, 1993. pp. 10.

7 洪郁芬《華文俳句選》，台北市，釀出版，二○一八年，一百四十頁。

8 今田述〈世界の「俳句・ハイク」事情〉，國際俳句交流協會，二○一八年九月十九日取自：http://www.haikuhia.com/about_haiku/world_info/China/how_to_create/intro.html

9 洪郁芬《華文俳句選》，台北市，釀出版，二○一八年，一百四十頁。

10 洪郁芬《華文俳句選》，台北市，釀出版，二○一八年，一百四十三頁。

11 五島高資〈国際俳句において最も大事な要素としての「切れ」〉。俳句大學*HAIKU* vol.1，二○一七年，十六頁。

12 洪郁芬《華文俳句選》，台北市，釀出版，二○一八年，一百四十四頁。

13 Jane Reichhold. *Writing and Enjoying Haiku.* USA:Kodansha, 2002, pp.31.

14 洪郁芬《華文俳句選》，台北市，釀出版，二○一八年，一百四十四頁。

15 永田滿德、吳衛峰、洪郁芬、趙紹球、郭至卿合著《華文俳句選》，台北市，釀出版，二○一八年。

序二

俳句は生活に忙しい現代人にとって、立ち留まって物を考えるひとつの良き習慣です。詩人はよく詩をダンスに例えます。詩がダンスであれば、俳句は文字で光を表現する文芸であると思います。心の聯想、そして感動を二行、または何文字かで表す瞬間の光。そんな俳句のナチュラルで、会心一笑するシンプルさに魅力を感じます。瞬間の感動と直接な名詞表現を特徴とする俳句は、二、三年前から現代詩を書く私にとって新たなる挑戦でした。[1]。現代詩との違いに試行錯誤しながら、だんだん季語一つで、瞬間の感動を捉える俳句を書けるようになりました。

俳句を学んでいくうちに、俳句は日本の日常芸術にとどまらず、世界中でブームになっていることを知りました。写像主義詩人、例えばフランスのポール=ルイ・クーシュー（Paul-Louis Couchou）、エズラ・パウンド（Ezra Pound）、そし

019

てメキシコのノーベル賞受賞者、オクタビオ・パズ（Octavio Paz）、そして近年ノーベル賞を受賞されたスウェーデンのトーマス・トランストロンメル（Thomas Tranströmer）も俳句を書きます。国際俳句社『Haiku Column』で発表している詩人は、イギリス、アメリカ、フランス、イタリア、ベルギー、ルーマニア、カナダ、インド、パキスタン、台湾など、世界中から来ています。要するに、俳句のグローバル化は私たちの想像を既に超えています。

台湾の俳句発展は戦前、そして戦中の日本語教育に始まります。十年ほど前に、日本語教育を受けた黄霊芝は愛媛県の正岡子規国際俳句賞を受賞されました。黄霊芝と十字詩の創立者である詹冰の後の台湾の俳句は、十文字の減字定型俳句、五七五の形式、日本語で書く俳句、そして三行の現代詩を俳句と呼ぶ、俳句新詩などの形で書かれてきました。俳句は日本語と英語の音節の違いで、一、二行のものもありますが、三行が主流になっています。

中国の漢俳の創立者、林林が主張するように、漢俳は五七五の形式のみであってはなりません。俳句の中身を日本俳句の中身に近づけるべきです。今までの三行俳句、五七五、そして季語を重んじる俳句が、果たして日本の俳句の精

020

神を表しているかどうかは疑わしいです[10]。俳人五島高資の論文によりますと、国際俳句において最も大事な要素は「切れ」で、五七五でも季語でもありません[11] [12]。なぜならば、一年中同じ季節の国もあり、また、それぞれの言葉はそれぞれ固有の韻律を持つからです。『*Writing and Enjoying Haiku*』の第二の規則[13] [14]によりますと、「俳句の形式で大切なのは、意味が二部に分かれていることです。なぜならば、俳句は三段切れと一物仕立てであってはならないからです。切れ、または止めで、一句の俳句を二部にするのです。」私たちが二〇一八年の十二月に出版した『華文俳句選』は、俳句の大切な美学である「切れ」と「取り合わせ」を実践しました。台湾の俳句と華文俳句の発展の詳細は、『華文俳句選』を参考して下さい[15]。

この百句の句集を出版するにあたり、華文俳句社の社長である洪郁芬女史に大いに励まされ、大変感謝しております。

この『凝光初現』は、中、日、英の三か国語で、世界に華文俳句を推進する始まりです。私の俳句を学習した心得を、俳句を書く人、または俳句をまだ知らない人と分かち合えば幸いです。他の文学形式よりも、生活の中で華文俳句のシン

021

プルな美しさを分かって頂けば嬉しいです。俳句を書くことは、シンプルかつ芸術的な生き方です。

二〇一九年五月吉日

郭至卿

CONTENTS

春

Spring

窗外盛開的紫藤

愛情小說

窓外に溢れんばかりの藤

恋愛小説

blossoming wisteria outside the window

a romance novel

鏡裏梳髮的女人
池塘邊的柳樹

鏡の中で髪をとかす女
池岸の柳

She's combing hair in the mirror
willow trees by the pond

春光
未加框的風景畫
春の光
額縁のなき風景画

spring light
unframed landscape

春曉
遠處傳來村莊的雞啼

春曉や
遠くの村より鶏の鳴き

spring dawn

chicken crowing from the village far away

春午
陽明山公園的寫生紙上一片紅一片綠

春の昼
陽明山公園で写生の紙に赤と緑

spring afternoon
the red and green drawing paper at Yang Ming Shan park

女孩銀鈴的笑聲
春天的花園

女子の銀鈴のような笑い声
春野原

the girl's silvery laugh
spring garden

春意濃
台北時裝展模特兒伸展台上走秀

春深し
台北のファッションショーで歩くモデル

deep spring

Taipei fashion show models are walking on the stage

麗日
禱告中浮現上帝的花園

麗らかや
祈りの中に浮かぶ神の花園

a glorious day

God's garden appeared in my prayer

桌上未拆的情書
含苞的鬱金香

机の上に閉じたラブレター
チューリップの蕾

unopened love letters on the table
budding tulips

曚朧夜色
陽明山石椅上的情侶

朧げな夜
陽明山の石椅子のアベック

hazy night

couples on stone bench at Mt. Yang Ming

媽祖祭
閱讀先民開墾的血淚史

媽祖祭
古代庶民の血と涙の開墾史を読む

Mazu Fete

read the tragic developmental history of the ancients

雲靄
未乾的潑墨山水畫

霞雲
乾かぬ溌墨の山水画

hazy clouds
splashing ink painting is undried

乍暖還寒
診所候診區客滿的病患

寒戻る
クリニックいっぱいの患者

turned cold again

patients filled up the clinic waiting room

翻開蒙上灰塵的舊相簿
窗戶上清明的細雨

灰を被ったアルバムを開く
窓に清明の小雨

open the dusty old album
Pure Brightness drizzle on the window

春宵
手握紅酒杯的耳邊私語

春の宵
ワイングラスを手にして話す耳元

spring night
holding a red wine glass and whisper

穿春裝的女郎
巴黎的陽光

春ドレスを著た女性
パリの日差し

a girl wearing a spring dress
sunshine in Paris

春耕
感恩讚歌的五線譜

春耕や
謝恩賛歌の五線譜

spring ploughing
a sheet music of thanksgiving hymn

遠足
特別早起的孩子

遠足
いつもより早起きの子

excursion

she gets up early today

春陰
難民潮移動的新聞

春陰や
移動する難民の群れのニュース

a hazy sky
news of moving refugee flows

春山笑
老夫婦牽手散歩

山笑ふ
老夫婦が手をつないで散歩する

laughing mountain
an old couple holding hands for a walk

薔薇芽
白紙上的詩題

薔薇の芽
白い紙に詩のタイトル

rose bud
a poem title on the white paper

務農的雙手
白盤裡蘆筍的翠綠

農民の手
白い皿にアスパラガスの青さ

hands of farmers
verdancy of asparagus in white porcelain plate

春天教堂的鐘聲
鴿子飛過的天空

春の教会の鐘
鳩が空を飛ぶ

bells of the church in spring

pigeons flew over the sky

鹿野高台上升的熱氣球
揮手的幼子

鹿野高台より上がる熱気球
手を振る幼子

rising hot air balloons on the Lu Ye stage

kids waving on the grass

春江
數算流動的雲朵
春の川
流れる雲を数える

spring river
counting flowing clouds

春泥上的腳印
爬蟲深陷

春泥の足跡
はまり込む虫

footprints on the spring mud
a bug is trapped

春泥上的腳印
爬蟲深陷

春泥の足跡
はまり込む虫

footprints on the spring mud
a bug is trapped

肥皂泡的虹彩
空中的調色盤

玉虫色のしゃぼん玉
空のパレット

iridescence of soap bubbles

palette in the air

詩人執筆的手不停啊！
春潮

詩人の筆は止まらない
春の潮

The pen in the poet's hand has never stopped
spring tide

坐岸邊的老人揮釣桿
水亦暖

岸辺の老人は釣竿を振る
水温む

an old man is casting a fishing rod

warming of water

復活節
看到空墓穴

復活祭
空の墓穴を見つけた

Easter
I found an empty tomb

春塵
低頭行走的駱駝隊伍

春の塵
俯きに歩くラクダの列

spring dust

a line of camels lowered their head and walked

石頭上翻開的園藝書
播花種

石の上に開いた園芸の本
花種蒔く

The book of gardening was opened on the stone
sowing flower seeds

漁船順東風歸來
岸邊煙裊裊

東風で帰ってきた漁船
岸辺に渦巻く煙

a fishing boat is back by the east wind
spiralling smoke in the shore

宜蘭童玩藝術節　彩色小風車
宜蘭童玩芸術祭
多色の風車

Yilan Children's Folklore & Folkgame Festival

small colorful windmills

春雨
閱讀連載的愛情小說

春の雨
シリーズの恋愛小説を読む

spring rain
reading serial love stories

女高音演唱會
山谷傳來的黃鶯鳴叫

ソプラノリサイクル
山の谷から伝わる鶯の声

soprano concert
yellow warblers tweet from the valley

中午下課鈴響
櫻花蝦飯便當

昼の授業終わりのベル
桜海老のご飯弁当

class bell ringing at noon
sakura shrimp rice lunch box

悠閒
爺爺在至善園的長椅上餵貓

のどかさや
至善園の長椅子でお爺さんが貓を飼っている

peaceful

grandpa fed the cat on the bench in the Zhi Shan garden

夏

Summer

女人耳際的髮絲
手中花色的扇子

女の鬢の髮
手の中に花色の扇子

woman's hair by the ear
flower fan in her hand

薔薇花瓣掉落
桌上變味的紅酒

落ちる薔薇の花びら
気のぬけた赤ワイン

falling rose petals
stale red wine on the table

枱燈下的針線盒
慶祝母親節的歌聲

明かりの下の針箱
母の日を祝う歌声

sewing box under the lamp
sing to celebrate Mother's Day

扛餅乾屑的螞蟻群
輕騎兵進行曲

クッキーを運ぶ蟻の列
軽騎兵序曲

a team of ants carrying biscuit crumbs
Light Cavalry Overture

地震後形成的瀑布
破裂的相框

地震後の滝
割れたフオトフレーム

waterfall formed after the earthquake

a cracked photo frame

蝸牛背著房子
一生數算路邊的石頭

家を背負う蝸牛
生涯道ばたの石を数える

the snail carries the house
a life that counts the stones beside the road

窗外的牡丹
插一支花簪在髮髻上

窗外の牡丹
髪際に花の簪を

peony outside the window

plugged a flower hairpin on the bun

屋簷的梅雨
少女寫戀愛日記

軒の梅雨
少女は恋愛日記を書く

rainy season under the eaves
the girl is writing love diaries

白鷺鷥
綠川上的休止符

白鷺
綠川に休符

white egret
a pause on the green river

一聲雷
成績單上的紅字

雷鳴一つ
通信簿の赤字

sound of thunder
a deficit in the report card

輕摸孩子發燒的額頭
手作母親節卡片

子供の熱い額に触れる
手作りの母の日カード

touch the child's feverish forehead
handmade Mother's Day card

海天之際的晚霞
郵輪駛進基隆港的鳴笛聲

水平線の夕焼け
基隆港へ帆走する旅客船の汽笛

sunset glows on the horizon
sirens of the passenger ship going into the Keelung Port

烏來露營帳篷外的歌聲
炭火

烏来のテントの外に歌声
炭火

singings outside the camping tent in Wulai
charcoal fire

遠方的雷聲
懸疑小說的結局

遠雷
サスペンスの終わり

distant thunder
the ending of the suspense novel

故事的第一頁
共傘的情侶

物語の最初のページ
相合傘

first page of the story
share an umbrella

戸外教室
金龜蟲穿梭草叢

野外教室
草むらを行き交う黄金虫

outdoor classroom
scarabs shuttled in grass

躲迷藏的女士
遮陽傘

隱れん坊の女
白日傘

She plays hide and seek
a sunshade

涼亭裡彈奏琵琶
池塘的睡蓮

東屋で琵琶を弾く
池の睡蓮

play the Chinese lute in the bower
water lilies in the pond

午後打盹
冰淇淋車的鈴噹聲

午後の居眠り
チリリンとアイスクリームワゴン

afternoon snooze
the bell of the ice cream cart rang

孩童手拿蛋坐好
立夏

卵を持ってきちんと座る子
立夏

he holds an egg and sits properly

the beginning of summer

家人晚餐聊天
池塘邊雨蛙鳴

家族の晩御飯の雑談
池辺の雨蛙

family dinner chat
rain frogs by the pond

雷電
土裡爬蟲的騒動

いかづち
土の中で騒ぐ爬虫類

thunderbolt

the commotion of the crawler in the earth

秋

Autumn

妻子的嘮叨聲
啄木鳥不眠

妻の愚痴
眠らぬ啄木鳥

wife's nagging
a woodpecker that doesn't sleep

瓷杯裡的古酒
妻子燈下的縫紉

陶磁カップに古酒
ランプの下の妻の縫物

ancient wine in the porcelain cup
wife's sewing under the lamp

醸葡萄
撰寫回憶錄

発酵の葡萄
回顧錄を書く

fermented grapes
write a memoir

敗荷
夢見年老的自己

敗荷
夢の中に年老いた自分

torned lotus

the older me in my dream

秋的天空
詩人吟誦聲迴盪

秋の空
詩人の朗読響く

autumn sky

echoed sounds of the poet's reciting

秋雨綿綿
長詩的線裝書

秋の雨
糸で綴じた長い詩の本

continuous rain in autumn
a thread-bound book of long poems

小籠包
孩子蘋果的臉

小籠包
子どものりんごのような顔

small bun
the child's apple face

驚嘆號的台北一〇一大樓
秋日高空

驚嘆符の台北一〇一ビル
秋の空

Taipei 101 building is an exclamation mark
autumn sky

山月
寺廟的鐘聲和驚飛的鳥

山の月
寺の鐘に驚いて飛ぶ鳥

mountain moon

bell of the temple and the startled birds

星月夜
閱讀探險家的小說

星月夜
探検家の小説を読む

starry night
read the explorer's novel

秋風的街燈
路人拉高衣領快步走

秋風の街灯
襟を立てる歩行者

streetlights in the autumn wind

the passenger pulled up his collars

秋天的海
輪椅上望向遠方的老人

秋の海
車椅子で遠方を見る老人

autumn sea

the old man looked far away in the wheelchair

日照楓葉
奧萬大的樹林小屋

照紅葉
奧万大の森の小屋

sunshine on maple leaves
little cabins in the wood of Aowanda

燈籠燭火一明一滅
跪坐誦經

チカチカの燈籠
跪いて読経する

glittering lantern

kneel down and chant the sutras

老屋內傳出二胡聲
秋風

古家より二胡の楽音
秋の風

music of Erhu fiddle from the old house
autumn wind

學烹飪的妙齡妻子
新酒

料理習い初めの若妻
新酒

young wife is learning cooking
new wine

老人埋入漩渦的眼神
秋湖

老人は視線を渦に注視する
秋の湖

the old man focused on the eddy

autumn lake

秋風
斜倒路邊的碑石

秋の風
道端の斜めに倒れた碑石

autumn wind
a stone tilt fell down aslant at the road side

冬

Winter

老鷹高山上飛翔
巡視的國王

高山の上の鷹
視察する王様

eagle flies above high mountains
a patrolling king

嚴寒　詩篇的誕生

嚴寒
詩の誕生

severe cold
birth of a poem

拄著拐杖的老人
北風聲

杖を持つ老人
北風の音

an old man with a cane
sound of north wind

滑冰比賽
音樂盒上旋轉的木偶

スケートの試合
オルゴールの回る木の人形

skating competition
puppets spinning on the music box

救援隊傳來的消息
寒晴

救援隊のお知らせ
寒日和

a sunny day in cold winter

news from the rescue team

翻閲族譜
枯草老屋前
家系図をめくる
枯草と古家の前

dip into the genealogy
in front of the wilted grass and the old house

冰柱
亞瑟王的石中劍

冰柱
アーサー王の岩に刺さっている剣

icicle

Arthur king's sword in the stone

大雪
帽簷陰影的眼眸

大雪
帽子のつばの影の目

heavy snow

eyes under the hat's shadow

新娘跳華爾滋舞
池塘裡的天鵝

花嫁がワルツを踊る
池の白鳥

the bride is dancing waltz

swans in the pond

拱橋下的漣漪
鴛鴦

アーチ橋の下のさざ波
鴛鴦

ripples under the arch bridge
Mandarin ducks

119

荷鋤的農夫唱著歌
冒出土的白蘿蔔

鍬を肩に乗せた農夫の歌
土から出た大根

singing of the farmer with a hoe
white radish popped up from the ground

蘭陽平原的冬天
山邊農舍的炊煙

蘭陽平原の冬
山辺に農舎の炊煙

Lan Yang plain in winter

farmhouses' smoke beside the mountains

樹下堆疊的俳句
落葉

木の下で積み重ねた俳句
落ち葉

haiku stacked under the tree
fallen leaves

溫酒香
妻子的髮髻

熱燗の香り
妻の髻

warm wine
wife's bun

滑雪
白紙上的素描

スキー
白い紙のスケッチ

skiing
sketch on the white paper

舞孃甩動大蓬裙
冬夜小酒館的吉他

ダンサーはパニエスカートを振る
冬のバーのギター

the dancer is shaking her panier skirt
guitar in the winter bar

土裡烤地瓜
稻草堆間奔跑的孩子

土の中の焼き芋
堆い稲穂の間を走る子供

sweet potatoes roasted in the soil
running children between the straw stacks

火爐旁的沙發上爺爺打瞌睡
桌上的圍棋

囲炉裏端のソファで居眠りするお爺さん
机の上の囲碁

grandfather dozing on the sofa next to the stove
game board go on the table

127

孩子張大的嘴
聖誕禮物的夜晚

子供の大きく開けた口
クリスマスプレゼントの夜

a big mouth of the kid
the night of Christmas present

枯野
亂石堆疊的塚

枯野原
乱れた石の塚

desolate field

a tomb stacked with rumpled stones

祖母戴著繡花帽
山櫻

刺繡の帽子を被ったお婆さん
山桜

grandma's wearing an embroidered hat

wild cherry blossoms

寒流至
二次大戰的紀念碑

寒波来る
第二次大戦の記念碑

cold stream comes

monument of the World War II

附錄一 日本著名俳人五島高資評郭至卿俳句三首

女子の銀鈴のような笑い声

春野原

日本の古代伝説における佐保姫を思い出す。秋の女神である竜田姫と対を成す春の女神である。日本神話では、「笑い」が重要な要素を担っている。天岩戸に隠れた天照大御神を再びお出まし願う際も神々の笑いが大きな役割を果たした。また、「笑う」は「咲く」に通じて春の開花とも共鳴する。ところで、史記において詩歌に重要とされ、また、俳句の三大要素の一つである「滑稽」は、「笑い」と深く関係している。理屈や意味を超克して深い共感に根ざす「笑い」はまさに銀の鈴のように貴いのである。

女孩銀鈴的笑聲

春天的花園

我想起日本古代傳說的佐保姬。春天的女神，常與秋天的女神龍田姬並肩而行。在日本神話裡，「笑」有舉足輕重的作用。例如，為了召喚躲在天岩戶的天照大御神，眾神的笑聲擔任了重要角色。另外，「笑」與「開」相通，與春天的花開產生共鳴。話說回來，史記記載詩歌的重要要素，也是俳句三大要素之一的「滑稽」與「笑」之間有很深的關聯。超越一切的道理和意義，根植於深沉共鳴的「笑」，確實如銀鈴般的珍貴。

復活祭

空の墓穴を見つけた

日本の『竹内文書』には、青森県戸来村（現・三戸郡新郷村大字戸来）にある

「十来塚」がイエス・キリストの墓と記されている。同書によれば、刑死したのはイエスの弟・イスキリであり、イエスは難を逃れて日本に逃げてきたとある。

伝説といえども、旧戸来村には、イエスに関連する文物が多く残っていて興味深いものがある。揭句の墓穴がイエスのものであるならばまさに「空」だったことも頷ける。このような伝説を知らなくても人々の無意識の中にキリストは生きているのである。

復活節
找到空墓穴

根據日本的『竹內文書』，青森縣戶来村（現今三戶郡新鄉村大字戶來）的「十來塚」是耶穌基督的墳墓。根據此書，被釘死在十架上的是耶穌基督的弟弟，而耶穌基督為了逃難來到日本。這雖然只是個傳說，戶來村自古以來確實殘留許多與耶穌基督相關的文物。若此俳句的墓穴是耶穌基督的，無庸置疑，那一定是空的。就算不曾耳聞這樣的傳說，耶穌基督也在人們的意識之外存在著。

東風で帰ってきた漁船
岸辺に渦巻く煙

古代、秦の始皇帝は東方海上に不老不死の島・蓬莱を探したとされる。中国の東方には、台湾はもちろん日本などの島嶼があるが、いずれも蓬莱伝説を持つ。かつて魏の文帝・曹丕は、「文章は経国の大業にして、不朽の盛事なり」と述べた。ここで俳諧精神を鑑みるとその出自は記紀歌謡にまで溯り、現代の俳句へと連なっている。これはまさに不朽の盛事であり、蓬莱の不老不死と相通じる。東方海上から帰った船が停泊する港町には、単なる生死を超えた精神文化が息づいているのだ。それは日常茶飯のなかに見いだされる俳諧精神として俳句に開示されるのである。

漁船順東風歸來
岸邊煙裊裊

據說古代的秦始皇於東方的海尋找長生不老的蓬萊仙島。中國的東方是台灣和

日本的島嶼，而這些地方都流傳此蓬萊傳說。過去魏文帝曹丕曾說：「文乃經國

之大業，不朽之盛事。」若我們探討俳諧精神，便可理解其可追溯至記紀歌謠的年

代，並流傳直至現代的俳句。這真是不朽的盛事，與蓬萊的長生不老有異曲同工之

處。順著東風歸來的船，停泊的港口有超越生死的精神文化。而這文化正以蘊藏於

日常生活的俳諧精神的姿態，展現在此俳句中。

五島高資氏プロフィール

日本俳句協会副会長、日本文芸家協会会員、現代俳句協会会員、日本現代詩歌

文学館振興会会員、日本内科学会会員、岩手県立千厩病院血液内科長、日本血液

学会会員、国際俳句交流協会会員、宇都宮国際文化協会会員、国立博物館特別支

援者、城見ヶ丘大学講師、俳句大学副学長、宇都宮大学非常勤講師。「全国学生

俳句大会推薦大賞兼文部大臣奨励賞」、「第十三回現代俳句新人賞」、「第十九

回現代俳句評論賞」、第一句集『海馬』にて中新田俳句大賞スウェーデン賞を受

賞。句集に『海馬』（東京四季）、『雷光』（角川書局）、『五島高資句集』（文学の森）、『蓬萊紀行』（富士見書房）。「俳句スクエア」代表。

五島高資先生簡歷

日本俳句協會副會長，日本文藝家協會會員，現代俳句協會會員，日本現代詩歌文學館振興會會員，日本內科學會會員，岩手縣立千廄醫院血液內科長、日本血液學會會員、國際俳句交流協會會員、宇都宮國際文化協會會員、國立博物館特別支援者、城見ヶ丘大學講師、俳句大學副校長、宇都宮大學特約講師。曾獲「全國學生俳句大會推薦大賞兼文部大臣獎勵賞」、「第十三回現代俳句新人獎」、「第十九回現代俳句評論賞受賞」、第一句集《海馬》獲「瑞典獎」。著有句集《海馬》（東京四季）、《雷光》（角川書局）、《五島高資句集》（文學之森）、《蓬萊紀行》（富士見書房）。網路「俳句スクエア」代表。

137

附錄二 華文俳句的寫作方法

華文俳句（以下簡稱「俳句」）的寫作方法說明如下：

一、俳句無題，分兩行。

例：

古池啊！
青蛙跳入水聲響

※松尾芭蕉（1644-1694）

二、第一行和第二行之間意思斷開，即日本俳句的「切」。二行間的關係，我們稱之為「二項組合」。二者不即不離，一重一輕，一主一次，由相互的關聯、襯托、張力來營造詩意。

例：

地球彷彿那方

魚鱗雲

※洪郁芬

三、我們提倡一首俳句用一個季語，即表示季節的詞語。

例：

秋日高空

驚嘆號的台北一○一大樓

※郭至卿

四、俳句內容須吟詠當下、截取瞬間。不寫過去和將來。

例：

蜻蜓點水

釣竿動也不動

※趙紹球

五、吟詠具體的事物。不寫抽象。

例：

浮世畫的逆捲波

早春還寒

※永田滿德

六、提倡簡約、留白。儘量不用多餘或說明性的詞語。

　例：

龍王出入的雲霄

青嶺

　　　　　　　　　　　　　　　　　　　　　※五島高資

　　　　　　　　　　　　　　　　　二〇一九年七月吉日

　　　　　　　　洪郁芬、郭至卿、趙紹球、吳衛峰

付録二　華文俳句の書き方

以下、華文俳句を俳句と称して説明する。

（一）俳句にタイトルはない。二行に書く。

　　例：

　　　古池や

　　蛙飛び込む水の音

　　　　　　　　　　※松尾芭蕉（1644-1694）

（二）一行目と二行目の間に切れがある。二行の関係は取り合わせで、つかず離れず、共に詩意を醸し出す。

例：

うろこ雲

向こうに地球あるやうな

※洪郁芬

（三）一句の俳句に季語一つを提唱する。

例：

驚嘆符の台北一〇一ビル

秋の空

※郭至卿

（四）今を読む。瞬間を切り取る。

　例：
　水面をかすめる蜻蛉
　動かぬ釣り竿

　　　　　　　　　　　　※趙紹球

（五）具体的な物を詠む。

　例：
　浮世絵の波の逆巻き
　寒戻る

　　　　　　　　　　　　※永田満徳

144

（六）用語は少なく。

　例：
　わたつみの雲居に通う
　青嶺かな

※五島高資

二〇一九年七月吉日

洪郁芬、郭至卿、趙紹球、吳衛峰

CONTENTS

Preface I

Same as the international department of Japan Haiku University who advocates "Cut" and "Toriawase", the Taiwanese publication of *First Ray of Light*, Kuo Chih Ching's personal Chinese haiku anthology, is worth celebrating.

Haiku is one of the traditional Japanese poetry. Now crossing the Japanese fence, haiku is written in different languages around the world, and has become an international literary style. However, looking at the reality of international haiku, we observe that most of the international haikus are written in three lines without the manifestation of the essence of haiku aesthetics. This is because the international haiku did not reach a consensus on the form and characteristics of haiku.

In order to promote "Cut" and "Toriawase (Juxtaposition)", which are the essence of haiku in the Chinese circle, I worked as a consultant and co-author of *Chinese Haiku Selection* in the publication of Yuhfen Hong, Kuo Chih Ching, Steven Chew and

Wu Weifeng in December 2018. In addition, I also served as a consultant to the "Chinese Haiku Society", which was established on December 4, 2018, to promote the development of Chinese Haiku.

As a consultant to the "Chinese Haiku Society", I am quite happy to see Kuo Chih Ching published *First Ray of Light*. I hope that the publication of this Chinese haiku anthology will enable readers to better understand the haiku aesthetics of "Cut" and "Toriawase." I hope that Chinese Haiku can work with classical poetry, modern poetry, short poetry and prose poetry to enrich the circle of Chinese poetry.

The first time I met Kuo Chih Ching, it was through her haiku "the girl's silvery laugh/ spring garden". The comment I gave her was "Good haiku!" She seemed to be motivated to join the ranks of writing haiku. In the process of constant trying, she seemed to understand the use of a Kigo (seasonal word) to capture the mystery of the moment of life.

From the outstanding contents of this Chinese Haiku Anthology, such as "The pen in the poet's hand has never stopped / spring tide", or "starry night / read the explorer's novel", we could see that Kuo Chih Ching loves reading and has outstanding literary

qualities and talents. Here I introduce several haikus published by Kuo Chih Ching in Japan *Kumagawa Syunsyuu* magazine:

> sound of thunder
> a deficit in the report card

It is probably the scene of registering the report cards of students when thundering. The light of thunder and the red of the transcript make a vivid contrast.

> an old man with a cane
> sound of north wind

At first glance, there seems to be no direct connection between "old man" and "north wind". Even so, we can still feel that the old man with a cane is standing against the cold north wind.

> spring light
> unframed landscape

"Spring light" here means "dazzling and soft light of spring."

Using the wording "unframed", clearly depicts the beautiful mountain landscape in spring that stretches as far as the eyes can see.

The color contrast of "sound of thunder" is quite good. In the haiku of "the old man with a cane", "old man" and "north wind" have a relationship that is not inseparable and just right. The haiku of "spring light" uses the technique of "Sketching". These haikus use "Cut" and "Toriawase", and are all better than most of the Japanese haikus. Finally, I list here the haikus that I admire:

blossoming wisteria outside the window
a romance novel

an old man is casting a fishing rod
warming of water

spring rain
reading serial love stories

distant thunder
the ending of the suspense novel

afternoon snooze
the bell of the ice cream cart rang

starry night
read the explorer's novel

Taipei 101 building is an exclamation mark
autumn sky

autumn sea
the old man looked far away in the wheelchair

a sunny day in cold winter
news from the rescue team

cold stream comes
monument of the World War II

July, 2019
Mitsunori NAGATA
Vice President of Japan Haiku Association

Presentation of Mitsunori NAGATA

Born in Japan, 1954. Vice President of Japan Haiku Association, President of Haiku University, editor of *Kasin* haiku quarterly, administrative secretary of Japan Haijin Association. Collections of haiku: *Kanmaturi*. Co-author of *100 Souseki Kumamoto* and *New Kumamoto Saijiki*.

Preface II

About First Ray of Light

For most of us, haiku can be a way to slow down our pace in our modern busy lives.

As the poets have said, "Poetry is to prose as dancing is to walking," I think haiku is an artistic performance that uses words to create the image of streaming light. The very light that shines beneath the surface of two lines or a few words enlightens a life where we choose not to pursue any goal, and a mental association and moving feeling of everything we see. What really attracts me to haiku is its unadorned beauty and its spontaneous form of writing which leads to an outpouring of smiles. I started to write modern poetry two or three years ago. Unlike modern poetry, haiku captures the moving moment with direct nouns. It was a tough challenge for me. [1] When attempting to write haiku, I gradually realized the subtle meaning of why Kigo (seasonal words) are used to praise the moving moments of our daily lives.

Becoming a global trend

When I was learning haiku, I also learned that the development of haiku has become a global trend. Haiku goes well beyond the art of Japanese daily life. Many world famous poets have written haiku, including Paul-Louis Couchoud and Ezra Pound, the representative poets of Imagism, Octavio Paz, the Mexican winner of Nobel Prize in Literature, and Thomas Tranströmer, the Nobel Prize winner in Literature.[2] Moreover, the "Haiku Column" has been joined by poets from various countries, including the United Kingdom, the United States, France, Italy, Belgium, Romania, Hungary, Canada, India, Pakistan, and Taiwan.[3] In brief, the development of haiku has globalized beyond our imagination.

The development of haiku in Taiwan originated from Japanese language education under colonial rule and during World War II. Over a decade ago, Mr. Huang Ling-zhi, who received a Japanese education, won the Masaoka Shiki International Haiku Award of Japan's Ehime Prefecture. [4]

The Development of Haiku in Taiwan

After Mr. Huang Ling-zhi's contribution to haiku , another

great poet, Zhan Bing, created the ten-character poem on the basis of haiku and simplified a haiku to within ten characters. Some poets wrote poems in the form of Japanese haiku, 5-7-5. In addition, three-line haiku called the new poetry of haiku, has been written by severals. [5]

Due to the difference between English and Japanese syllables, there are haikus written in one or two lines, though most English haikus still use three lines. [6,7]

One of the founders of Chinese haiku, Mr. Lin Lin, also suggested that Chinese haiku should not be confined to the form of 5-7-5. However, the connotation still need to adhere to the original Japanese haiku. [8,9]

Besides, it is still under debate whether the written form of 5-7-5 and three lines or seasonal words could truly express the core spirit of Japanese haiku. [10]

In a paper written by Japanese Haijin Takatoshi GOTO, he emphasizes that the most vital thing about haiku is Kire (Cut), rather than Kigo (seasonal words) or the 5-7-5 form after all, because some countries only have a single season. Moreover, different languages do not share the same rhythm.

Writing and Enjoying Haiku

In the 2nd point of Six Principles of English Haiku mentioned in *Writing and Enjoying Haiku* [13,14]: "The most important part of writing a haiku is to separate the expression into two parts, since haiku cannot be cut into three parts or be written in just a plain sentence. There has to be a cut or pause in the middle of a line, separating the line into two parts."

Chinese Haiku Anthology, published in December, 2018, focused on using Kire (Cut) and Toriawase (juxtaposition) to express the true nature of haiku. If you are interested in Taiwan or Chinese development of haiku, please refer to the *Chinese Haiku Anthology*. [15]

During the writing of 100 haikus, Ms. Yuhfen Hong, Director of the Chinese Haiku Society, gave me advice and courage, and hence, thanks to her patience and support, I was able to finish this compilation. I express my gratitude toward Ms. Yuhfen Hong!

First Ray of Light is published in three languages, Chinese, English and Japanese, which is a new start for global promotion of haiku. Throughout the book, I would like to share what I've learned from haiku with those who are writing one or to those who are

unfamiliar with it. Also, I hope that this book can attract the attention of people speaking various languages, and provide them a wonderful chance to experience pure beauty from different aspects, one better than that from other forms of literature. Finally, writing haiku is an easy and inexpensive way to achieve a life of art for everyone.

References

[1] 吳衛峰《華文俳句選》，台北市，釀出版，2018年，13頁。

[2] 川本皓嗣《華文俳句選》，台北市，釀出版，2018年，3頁。

[3] 永田満德《華文俳句選》，台北市，釀出版，2018年，151頁。

[4] 川本皓嗣《華文俳句選》，台北市，釀出版，2018年，4頁。

[5] 洪郁芬《華文俳句選》，台北市，釀出版，2018年，140頁。

[6] Bruce Rose ed.,*HAIKU MOMENT*. USA:Tuttle Publishing, 1993. pp. 10.

[7] 洪郁芬《華文俳句選》，台北市，釀出版，2018年，140頁。

[8] 今田述〈世界の「俳句・ハイク」事情〉，國際俳句交流協會，2018年9月19日取自：http://www.haikuhia.com/about_haiku/world_info/China/how_to_create/intro.html

[9] 洪郁芬《華文俳句選》，台北市，釀出版，2018年，140頁。

[10] 洪郁芬《華文俳句選》，台北市，釀出版，2018年，143頁。

[11] 五島高資〈国際俳句において最も大事な要素としての「切れ」〉。俳句大學*HAIKU* vol.1,2017,16頁。

[12] 洪郁芬《華文俳句選》，台北市，釀出版，2018年，144頁。

[13] Jane Reichhold. *Writing and Enjoying Haiku*. USA:Kodansha, 2002, pp.31.

[14] 洪郁芬《華文俳句選》，台北市，釀出版，2018年，144頁。

[15] 永田満德、吳衛峰、洪郁芬、趙紹球、郭至卿合著《華文俳句選》，台北市，釀出版，2018年。

Epilogue I -
Commentary on Kuo Chih Ching's Haiku by Takatoshi GOTO

the girl's silvery laugh

spring garden

I recall the Japanese ancient legend, SAHOHIME. She rules the entire Spring, corresponded to Autumn Goddess, TATSUTAHIME. In the ancient Japanese myth, "laugh" has an important effect. For example, in order to summon the God of Sun, AMATERASU who hidden in the Amano-iwato, laughing of other Gods' play an important role. Moreover, "laugh" equals to "opening", resonate to blooming of spring. In any case, there is a deep connection between the key element described in the historical poem or story, and "Comic", one of the three key elements of Haiku. Beyond any reasons and meanings, deeply resonated "laugh" is precious as silver bells.

Easter

I found an empty tomb

Based on Japanese historical fantasy *Takeuchimonzyo*, Jesus' grave is located at Aomori Herai village. The book also described that Jesus Christ was escaped to Japan, and his brother was crucified instead of him. Although it is only a legend, the village indeed obtains lots of relics concerning Jesus Christ. If the "tomb" of this haiku is actually Jusus' tomb, the reality may be an empty tomb. People may never heard of this legend, but Jesus indeed, exists beyond our awareness.

a fishing boat is back by the east wind

spiralling smoke in the shore

Based on Chinese legend, the first emperor Qin was looking for immortal secret at Penglai island, east sea of mainland China. Where are Japan and Taiwan now, with Penlai legends anywhere. Emperor Cao Yu of the Wei dynasty quoted, "The literature is the foundation of governing, and also an event of immortal". If we

trace the spirit of poem, it will lead us to the historical ancient age, spreads toward concurrent haiku. This indeed is an event of immortal, legendary as Penglai legend. Followed by the east wind, fishing boat returning to the port, has never ending spiritual culture, beyond birth and death. The culture shows up in this haiku, as spirit of haiku in everyday life.

Presentation of Takatoshi GOTO

Born in Nagasaki city, Japan, May 23, 1968. Graduated from Jichi Medical University. Vice President of Japan Haiku Association, President of Haiku Square, editor of Monthly *Haiku World*, Vice President of Haiku University, member of Japanese Artists Association. Won the Nakashinden Sweden Haiku Prize in 1997, the Award for Modern Haiku Criticism in 2000 and so on. Collections of haiku: *Hippocampus*, *Thunderbolt* and so on.

Epilogue II - Writing Methods of Chinese Haiku

1. Chinese Haiku is untitled and is divided into two lines.

> e.g.
>
> old pond
>
> sound of a frog leaping into the water

※Matsuo Bashō (1644-1694)

2. The disconnection of meaning between the first line and the second line is the "Cut" of the Japanese haiku. The relationship between the two lines is what we call the "Toriawase." The poetry is created by mutual association, setting and tension.

e.g.

mackerel clouds

the earth is beyond

※Yuhfen Hong

3. We advocate one Kigo (seasonal word) in a haiku.

e.g.

Taipei 101 building is an exclamation mark

autumn sky

※Kuo Chih Ching

4. The content of a haiku must describe a moment at present. Do not
write the past and the future.

e.g.

a dragonfly skimming the surface of the water

still fishing rod

※Steven Chew

5. Write concrete things. Do not write abstractions.

e.g.

the reverse waves of Ukiyoe

early spring turned cold again

※Mitsunori NAGATA

6. Promote simplicity and leave blank. Try not to use redundant or descriptive words.

e.g.

blue mountains

Watatsumi comes and goes into the cloudy sky

※Takatoshi GOTO

July, 2019
Yuhfen Hong
Kuo Chih Ching
Steven Chew
Wu Weifeng

華文俳句叢書2　PG2329

 凝光初現
　　　——華文俳句集

作　　者	郭至卿
責任編輯	洪聖翔
圖文排版	周妤靜
封面設計	蔡瑋筠

出版策劃	釀出版
製作發行	秀威資訊科技股份有限公司
	114 台北市內湖區瑞光路76巷65號1樓
	電話：+886-2-2796-3638　傳真：+886-2-2796-1377
	服務信箱：service@showwe.com.tw
	http://www.showwe.com.tw
郵政劃撥	19563868　戶名：秀威資訊科技股份有限公司
展售門市	國家書店【松江門市】
	104 台北市中山區松江路209號1樓
	電話：+886-2-2518-0207　傳真：+886-2-2518-0778
網路訂購	秀威網路書店：https://store.showwe.tw
	國家網路書店：https://www.govbooks.com.tw
法律顧問	毛國樑　律師
總 經 銷	聯合發行股份有限公司
	231新北市新店區寶橋路235巷6弄6號4F
	電話：+886-2-2917-8022　傳真：+886-2-2915-6275

| 出版日期 | 2019年10月　BOD一版 |
| 定　　價 | 220元 |

Printed in Taiwan

國家圖書館出版品預行編目

```
凝光初現：華文俳句集 / 郭至卿作. -- 一版. --
臺北市：釀出版, 2019.10
    面；  公分. -- (華文俳句叢書；2)
BOD版
中日英對照
ISBN 978-986-445-349-8(平裝)

863.51                         108013953
```

讀者回函卡

感謝您購買本書，為提升服務品質，請填妥以下資料，將讀者回函卡直接寄
回或傳真本公司，收到您的寶貴意見後，我們會收藏記錄及檢討，謝謝！
如您需要了解本公司最新出版書目、購書優惠或企劃活動，歡迎您上網查詢
或下載相關資料：http:// www.showwe.com.tw

您購買的書名：_____

出生日期：_____年_____月_____日

學歷：□高中 (含) 以下　　□大專　　□研究所 (含) 以上

職業：□製造業　□金融業　□資訊業　□軍警　□傳播業　□自由業
　　　□服務業　□公務員　□教職　　□學生　□家管　　□其它_____

購書地點：□網路書店　□實體書店　□書展　□郵購　□贈閱　□其他

您從何得知本書的消息？

　□網路書店　□實體書店　□網路搜尋　□電子報　□書訊　□雜誌

　□傳播媒體　□親友推薦　□網站推薦　□部落格　□其他_____

您對本書的評價：(請填代號　1.非常滿意　2.滿意　3.尚可　4.再改進)

　封面設計____　版面編排____　內容____　文／譯筆____　價格____

讀完書後您覺得：

　□很有收穫　□有收穫　□收穫不多　□沒收穫

對我們的建議：_____

_____

_____

_____

11466
台北市內湖區瑞光路 76 巷 65 號 1 樓

秀威資訊科技股份有限公司　　　　收

BOD 數位出版事業部

⋯⋯⋯⋯⋯⋯⋯⋯⋯⋯⋯⋯⋯⋯⋯⋯⋯⋯⋯⋯⋯⋯⋯⋯⋯⋯⋯

（請沿線對折寄回，謝謝！）

姓　　名：_____　年齡：_____　性別：□女　□男

郵遞區號：□□□□□

地　　址：_____

聯絡電話：(日) _____ (夜) _____

E-mail：_____